Gersham and the Golem

Portrait of a Boy, Collection of the Jewish
Museum in Prague: Jewish Museum in Prague
Photo Archive

Gersham and the Golem

A novel by

Edwin M. Radin

proving
press

Book Design & Production: Columbus Publishing Lab
www.ColumbusPublishingLab.com

LCCN: 2019906416
Paperback ISBN: 978-1-63337-274-0
E-book ISBN: 978-1-63337-275-7

Printed in the United States of America
1 3 5 7 9 10 8 6 4 2

To my beautiful wife, Judy, and my mother, Sandra. Thank you for your patience, love, and support during my creative period while I was writing this book.

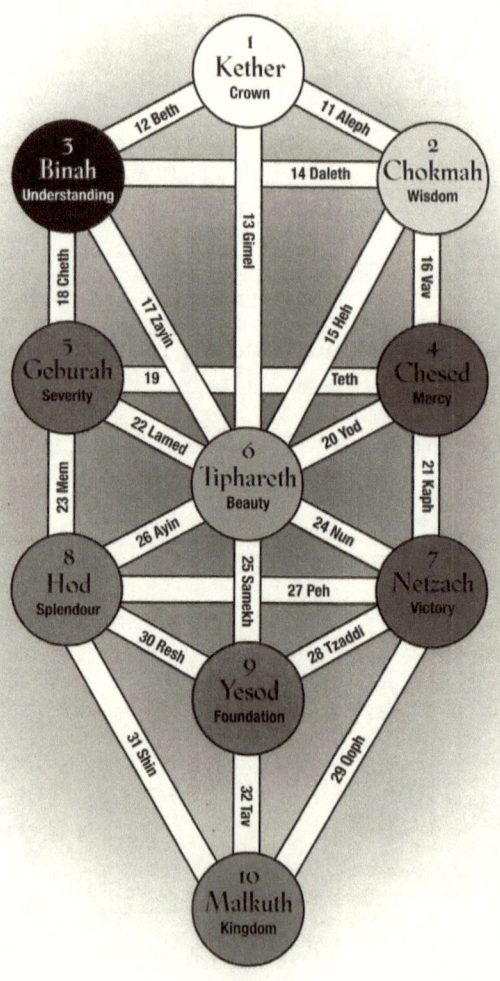

The Tree of Life

1 Kether
Crown

3 Binah
Understanding

2 Chokmah
Wisdom

12 Beth

11 Aleph

14 Daleth

13 Gimel

18 Cheth

17 Zayin

15 Heh

16 Vav

5 Geburah
Severity

4 Chesed
Mercy

19

Teth

22 Lamed

20 Yod

6 Tiphareth
Beauty

23 Mem

26 Ayin

24 Nun

21 Kaph

8 Hod
Splendour

25 Samekh

27 Peh

7 Netzach
Victory

30 Resh

28 Tzaddi

9 Yesod
Foundation

31 Shin

32 Tav

29 Qoph

10 Malkuth
Kingdom

PROLOGUE

What is the Kabbalah?

The Kabbalah is the ancient mystic wisdom of the Jewish faith. There are many parts to the Kabbalah. First, it is a map that shows the path to self-perfection. Second, it is an elegant model of the psyche. Third, it is God's blueprint for creation. It is all this and much more. It is a vibrant body of mystical techniques and teachings that can help unlock the true meaning of life, the universe, creation and, well, pretty much everything. The Kabbalah takes the form of a large body of teachings—written, oral, and practical—about the nature of God himself, the birth of the soul, the process of creation, and our purpose on earth. The Kabbalah also can explain life after death. There are specific techniques for improving the mind, body, and soul as well as life.

The Kabbalah does not try to identify or label God. Nor does it preach beliefs. Instead it assures the seeker that it is possible to experience God for oneself.

The Kabbalah came to be developed around three thousand

years ago, through the Kabbalistic ages of the twelfth through fifteenth centuries, and even into more modern times.

The Book of Splendor, or the Sepher ha-Zohar, is a masterpiece of Kabbalistic thought. It is made up of several thick volumes loaded with commentaries, thoughts, and lectures. It has brought out all the information and given the Kabbalah the written record it needed to gain more of an acceptance. When one wants to study the Kabbalah, the Zohar is considered a prerequisite to achieving any serious mastery of the Kabbalistic tradition.

The Kabbalah can put forth and possess amulets for prosperity, protection from evil and dark magic, love, luck, and good health. The literal translation of Kabbalah is "receiving." This refers to receiving the hidden mystical truths behind Jewish thinking and traditions. According to Kabbalistic traditions, knowledge of the Kabbalah was orally transmitted by the patriarchs and sages, in order to achieve full protection from black magic cast by witches and sorcerers. This novel is a story that starts in the mid-eighteenth century in Southern Poland with a Baal Shem, whom we'll refer to as both the Baal Shem and rabbi. *Baal Shem* is translated as "master of the word," a miracle worker, one who heals the sick, expels demons, and brings joy to his followers. The rabbi has a group of five students, who meet two to three days per week to study the Kabbalah. The youngest student, Gersham, is very bright and full of questions. Gersham wants to bring life to nothingness. He is obsessed with the idea and will do whatever it takes to find out how he can accomplish this.

Gersham and his friends, Esair, Joshua, and Abraham, along with the Rabbi (Baal Shem) and Jacob, the oldest teacher, all live in a small Jewish community in Southern Poland. The community consists of two main streets, back to back with homes on each side of the street. The homes are built side by side of stone and mortar and are four to a unit. The roofing is made from cobblestone to help the rain make its way down to the street below. Homes like this line both streets along with shops that sell everything from clothing to books, food, vegetables, and other necessities people could buy and use. Gersham's family owns the little bakery in the middle of town.

In the town square there is an old rundown, but stable, building that serves as their synagogue, also made of stone and mortar. The front of the synagogue has a very large wooden door with a beautiful Star of David, also known as a Mogen David, carved into it. The door stands eight feet tall and five feet wide. As you enter the synagogue, to the right you will find the sanctuary with an altar for the rabbi and rows of benches horizontally set in front of the altar. There is a small wooden ark behind the altar that holds the one Torah that the synagogue owns and a hanging fixture holding a large white candle. This is their eternal light, and it is Jacob's responsibility to light the candle before all services and holidays. To the left are two classrooms, including a library for study and a room that serves as the private office of the Rabbi. The rabbi's office is a small unit with a window on his right. There is a large tapestry hanging on the wall behind his desk, and a few old books sitting on a dusty shelf—mostly prayer books and stories about the Jewish religion.

To the right of the temple stands a fifteen-foot-tall round tower, again made from the same stone and mortar, with a large iron bell at the top that calls the community to prayer and also rings in the holidays as well as joyous occasions.

And finally, there is a back door to the temple, rarely used but kept unlocked for the scholars to come in and study during the week. All in all, it is a nice and comfortable little town where everyone gets along and serves the Lord.

This is the start of their Kabbalistic and mystical journey.

ONE

The year was 1747. It was a cold, snowy day in Southern Poland. As Israel Ben Shotsky looked out his window, the snow was coming down hard and everything was a beautiful, bright shade of white. The flakes were large and fluffy and glistened in the rays of the sun coming down on his part of the community in Southern Poland.

Israel Ben Shotsky was a man in his forties. He had long gray hair and bushy eyebrows and stood at six feet two inches tall. His long gray beard flowed from his chin. He always wore a long black flowing robe, and boots to keep his feet warm. Israel was a scholar and teacher at a small synagogue in Southern Poland. The temple was graced by fifty different families wanting to learn and pray for the better things in life. Israel was also the rabbi at this synagogue. He was fluent in the teachings of the Kabbalah and had a small group of students eager to learn its mystical teachings. There were five students who studied with the rabbi.

Israel Ben Shotsky was born into a Hassidic family. Besides his being a rabbi and teacher, he was also known the Baal Shem, or "miracle worker." He was born into poverty and rose to inspire the Jews in Southern Poland. Israel Ben Shotsky became known as the first and only Baal Shem Tov, "master of the good word." As a child, Israel was a very reluctant student. Instead of going to his classes at the synagogue, he would rather meditate with nature. There, he felt nature gave him a pure link to God. As he wandered, he became famous in his community for curing insanity as he frequently used Kabbalistic spells and amulets.

On this cold and snowy morning in February, the rabbi took his five students into the woods, and together they built a fire to sit around and keep warm as they talked. The oldest of his students was a tall, thin gentleman named Jacob. Being the oldest, he also led most of the classes and conversations between the group members. Jacob was a learned scholar, who like the Baal Shem continued to study and learn Kabbalah. The other members of the group were Esair, Joshua, Abraham, and Gersham. Gersham was the youngest, however very bright for his age of fourteen. He was also very inquisitive. He was more interested in the mystical side of Kabbalah and wanted to learn more about spells and amulets. Gersham stood at five feet five inches with short brown hair. He always wore his dark blue robe with a star and moon toward the bottom. On his head he always wore his fur-trimmed hat, called a shtreimel, over his yarmulke. His aspiration was to learn all he could and become a mystic within the Kabbalah. He also wore a gold chain around his neck with an amulet attached for good luck and good health.

The Baal Shem knew this and knew he had to keep an eye on Gersham so he wouldn't go down the dark path.

With everyone sitting around the fire, Jacob told the other students and the rabbi to look into the fire. Not only did the fire keep them warm, but the fire produced beautiful colors: reds, yellows, blues, and purples, along with a beautiful array of oranges. The fire pit was located below a beautifully shaped tree of many branches. Jacob decided it was the perfect time to talk about and study the Kabbalah's Tree of Life. Jacob was a scholar of the Kabbalah. He had sat and studied many nights with the Baal Shem, learning all he could about the Kabbalah. Jacob was twenty-two years old, six feet tall, and had long black hair with flowing streaks of silver, as well as a mustache and beard—not as long a beard as the Baal Shem, but very full just the same. Jacob wore a flowing black robe with a tallit around his neck. He also wore a kipah on his head, covered with a pointed black hat. He looked just like a wizard. Jacob adjusted his round wire-rimmed glasses and began the lesson.

"The Tree of Life," Jacob began, "is the master key for the gates of creation. It is the blueprint that underlies everything from the structure of the universe down to the way a human personality is created. The Tree of Life shows how the spark of divinity became the substance of the universe. It is the route from energy to matter, from God to man."

Gersham stood up, his face illuminated by the fire, and looked around at the forest and the surrounding nature.

"Jacob," he said. "This is very interesting. I would like to know more about this Tree of Life. Is it possible that we can bring something back to life using this tree?"

"There's a lot more to it than that," laughed Jacob. Joshua, Abraham, and Esair remained sitting, staring into the fire, eager to learn more about bringing back life to a dead object. Esair looked over at Gersham and asked him to quiet down with all his questions so that they could learn more about this Tree of Life from Jacob.

Gersham sat back down, saying very quietly, "I'm sorry. I won't interrupt anymore."

Jacob looked directly at Gersham. "Don't worry, my friend. The fact that you're asking questions shows that you are willing to learn and understand."

Jacob pressed on. "There are ten parts of the Tree of life, and many pathways between the parts. All parts of The Tree of Life become an aspect of the physical world: inanimate matter, human consciousness, physical actions, and even intangible ideas. The Tree of Life can circle all possibilities. Before the Tree of Life, it was just the infinity of God's divinity. Nothing else existed."

"Nothing?" said Joshua. "No planets, no nature, no humans, nothing?"

"Nothing," said Jacob. "Just one infinite void."

"Wow," said Joshua. "That is hard to imagine!"

"Just close your eyes," said Jacob. "Tell me what you see, Joshua."

"Nothing, absolutely nothing. Just darkness."

"Exactly," said Jacob. "Exactly."

Joshua was the same age as Gersham, but not as feisty. He wore a green robe with a deer at the bottom. Joshua had long brown hair with a hint of a mustache and beard.

"The first piece of the tree is called the Kether, or the Crown. Kether awakens to its own existence, and despite its consciousness, has no awareness.

"The second part," Jacob continued, "is known as the Sephira, or Wisdom. This formed in response to the Crown's unity. Also called Chokmah, it's able to look back at the crown and perceive the wonder of the divine love. These two parts provide the basis of the path. It is both the source and recipient of that energy and pushes the energy out joyfully. Here, God said, 'Let there be Light.'

"The third part of the tree is called the Binah, or the Womb of God. With the Binah's formation, movement and space become meaningful. Here, God said, 'Let the heavens expand.' To be a part of Binah is to be united with infinite understanding and awareness. Within its energies, are all intermixed and mingled, seamless for all intents and purposes, but each part of the whole remembers itself and retains its intangible connections.

"The fourth part," said Jacob, "is called Chesed, or Mercy. This part is in constant change. Everything is welcome here. There is the thought that there is a shortage of time and space, which does create some problems, however. Not everything is meant to exist. There is not enough room for everything. And it was here that God expanded the waters."

This time Esair raised his hand. "What happens," he said, "if something comes into this world and there's no space for it?"

Jacob answered this question the only way he could. "Well," he said, "this means that now something has to die for it to take its place."

"Like what?" asked Esair. "Like a tree, like a human, a flower, or an animal?"

Jacob looked down at Esair. "Death is a part of life," he said. "There is a plan that all life eventually will die when the time comes." This brought a lot of sighs from the other four students. Jacob pressed on.

"The fifth part is Geburah, or Severity. This part understands that some elements must be sacrificed to make way for other more appropriate things in life. Geburah is associated with the planet Mars and shares the same red color. It is the sphere of sacrifice, destruction, and loss. This sphere is one of the most important and most fundamentally misunderstood influences in the entire tree. Geburah has to be balanced and tempered by its opposite number, Chesed. Geburah and Chesed are opposite each other in the tree. These two spheres keep each other balanced. One cuts away excess and the other makes room for healthy growth and development. And God said, 'Let the earth put forth grass from the ground.'"

Jacob continued, "Number six, Tiferet, or Beauty—this is the home of the individual soul. Each living thing has a soul inside of it, which helps guide it through life."

Again, Gersham stood up. "If the soul is Beauty, why are there so many evil people in the world? Why do men start wars? Why all the killing?" Gersham yelled animatedly.

The other members of the group chimed in and wanted to know as well. Jacob sighed and said, "Each soul acts as a guide for the person; however, not every person listens to his or her soul. Such a person's thoughts are only of greed and the finer things in life, not caring about anyone else. This is why we study Kabbalah. This is why we learn Kabbalah. This is why we help and counsel other people to live better lives," explained Jacob. Each student stared into the fire, pondering each and every one of Jacob's words.

"Moving on," said Jacob. "The perfection of Tiferet gives birth to Netzach, the seventh part of the Tree of Life. Netzach is an engine of energy and direction. It's powered by the endless energy of divinity. This motion is both physical and spiritual and gives rise to emotion. Emotion is the force that drives the personality. This leads to part number eight, Hod, or Glory. This is the place of rational thought and scrutiny, and where communication becomes possible, because the personal mind is taking shape."

Joshua stood up and said, "So the way we communicate now is part of Hod. Each one here is thinking for himself. And Hod is helping our minds put together our words to carry on this conversation."

"Exactly," said Jacob. "It was also here that God said, 'Let the earth bring forth living creatures.'

"Number nine," Jacob continued, "is Yesod, or Foundation. This is the part of pure intelligence and is the first sphere that Malkuth connects with. It is the place of interface between the state of just being and the wisdom represented by the rest of the Tree. Yesod is described as pure intelligence because it is the final part of the rest of the Tree. This sphere is often identified with the moon. It grabs and reflects the light down to the surface of the earth. In other words, it is the sphere of the unconscious. It connects the past with the urgings and tendencies of the higher souls. It blends that material conscious thought and feeling. And it was here that God proclaimed, 'Let's make man.'

"Finally, the tenth part of the Tree of Life is Malkuth, or the

Kingdom. Malkuth created the universe, and the purpose of the tree is finally completed. This is the lowest of all the spheres. It is also known as Shekihnah, which refers to the female aspect of God. Malkuth represents the state of being. It is stability, the end result, physical embodiment—the very end of the act of creation. Malkuth is the realm of direct physical experience, the place where our senses interact with what is real. And," Jacob said, "this is where God said, 'Let all living things be fruitful and multiply.'"

Abraham finally raised his hand. "So God is both male and female?"

"Yes," said Jacob. "As it takes both a man and a woman to reproduce and start a family, God must be able to create, but in a different way."

"Interesting, very interesting," said Abraham. Abraham was seventeen years young and the quiet one of the group. He stood close to five feet ten inches and had long black hair. He also wore a beard much shorter than the rabbi's or Jacob's. However, he was working on it. His robe was a very dark green with a bright ball of light embroidered at the bottom. He also wore a kipah on his head. He awaited the day when he could start wearing robes of black. To do this he would have to graduate from Torah school, which would be in another couple of years.

As Jacob looked down at the fire, he noticed it was dying out. "It's getting late."

"Agreed," said the Baal Shem. "This is enough for the day. We shall carry on our conversation later."

With that said, the fire was put out and the students headed for home.

While walking home, Esair asked, "When will we meet again, Rabbi?"

"Three days from now we will again meet at the same place we met today and at the same time."

"OK," said Esair as he split from the group and headed home. "I'll see you all next time, and Good Shabbos everyone!" Esair was nineteen and wore a robe of purple and gold. He was the most flamboyant of the group. Esair was five feet seven inches and had long, flowing, rich mahogany-colored hair, which he tied back in a long ponytail to keep from blowing in his face. He had a long, dark beard and mustache and wore small round wire-rimmed glasses near the top of his nose, which made him look more like a wizard than a scholar. He was also one of the brightest and most knowledgeable of the group and always carried a leather-bound book in which he wrote many a note from the things he had learned.

Gersham walked slowly home thinking about all he had learned that day. From nothingness to creation was a lot for a fourteen-year-old to take in. But Gersham was not an ordinary young man. He was a very bright student who longed for more knowledge of Kabbalah, and more out of life.

TWO

Gersham finally arrived home, opened the door, and was greeted by the delicious aroma of freshly baked bread and Polish stew. It smelled so good that he couldn't wait to eat.

After washing up, he came down and sat at the dinner table with his parents and talked about the events of the day. Later, after dinner, his father served a little bit of plum brandy, also known as slivovitz, to celebrate the Sabbath day. Gersham was allowed only one shot. Then he helped clean up, said good night to his parents, and went off to bed.

As Gersham lay in his bed, he thought to himself how wonderful it would be to create something out of nothing. He really wanted to take a lump of earth or clay and bring it to life. He thought to himself, That day will come. I just need to learn more. Finally, he closed his eyes and went to sleep. Gersham had to get up early in the morning and help his father at the family bakery. He had challahs to bake and delicious buns to put out. Tomorrow was Shabbat, and as with every Friday, Shabbat was a big deal in his community. On Friday evening the jewish families celebrated the weekly holiday with a family meal and then everyone went to their synagogue for Shabbat services. There they prayed to God to thank him for the food we eat, the fruits of the vine and good health. Shabbat lasted from Friday at sundown to Saturday at dusk.

Sunday morning came and Gersham jumped out of bed, put on his robe, and jogged to the meeting place where he saw the rabbi and the other students collecting wood for another outdoor fire. They had plenty of wood to feed the fire and keep it going all day. Esair and Joshua had finished building the fire and gotten it started. Gersham found his place in the middle, between Joshua and Esair. It was another cloudy day, but today it was not snowing at all. There was a major chill in the air, but they all stayed warm near the fire.

After a long ten minutes, Jacob ended his conversation with the Baal Shem and got up to lead the class again. As he stood near the fire, he looked down at the other students trying to keep warm and then looked over at the Baal Shem.

"The other day," Jacob began, "we talked about the Tree of Life and all its parts. Today, I want to teach you the different paths you can take between the parts of the tree."

This got everyone's attention, especially Gersham's, who

forgot all about being cold. He thought to himself, Maybe one of these paths will lead me in the right direction to the creation of life from nothingness.

Jacob began by stating, "There are many paths you can take depending on where you want to go. There are many," he said, "but I will go over some of the more important paths. The first path is Malkuth to Yesod. God saw everything he made and rejoiced. He thought to himself, This is very good. Our personalities sense of self is caught between the objective reality of Malkuth and the imagination and unconsciousness of Yesod. It's the gate to the underworld and the path by which instinct is elaborated. Then there is Malkuth to Hod, the path to logic and logical thought. It is the home of the personality when it is consciously checking out a situation or an object. The rationalizations of Hod are taken down to Malkuth for actualization. The experience of Malkuth is carried up to Hod for analysis. Are you with me?" asked Jacob as he looked down at their puzzled faces. There was nothing but blank stares and silence.

Jacob smiled and continued. "Then there is a path from Yesod to Hod, which is the path of knowledge and understanding. When you read or speak in your native language, you do not have to decipher each word. When you toss a ball in the air and then try to catch it before it hits the ground, you do not have to work out any math to do it. You do it out of instinct and what you already know. Your body and mind work together, and it becomes a natural assimilation. Like walking—you learn at an early age, and from there it comes naturally." Jacob sensed he was getting somewhere now by the looks on their faces. He looked over at the Baal Shem and got a nod of approval.

Jacob continued. "There is a path from Yesod to Netzach, which is the path of intuition and harmony of the body, mind, and soul. Psychic forces come into play now. It is where the unconscious mind taps into a greater awareness of the universal energy. This is the path where humans can contact the gods and goddesses of legend, the source of psychic information, and find the personal connection to the will of the universe. To find your way here is to move in tune with the purpose of the universe."

"Now we're getting somewhere," Gersham said, louder than he wanted to.

Jacob just looked at him and smiled. He moved on. "There is the path from Hod to Netzach, the home of speech and meaning. It is the force that drives the abstract to seek materialization and solidification through the spoken word. This path is also known as the seat of magic—the art of causing change through intention."

This path took hold of Gersham. He thought, Magic! Keep talking, I want to learn more.

"Walking this path requires that your mind let go of its certainty and inflexibility. Some of the ideas you have must be allowed to disengage or fall off before new thoughts have the space to evolve.

"Next," Jacob continued, "is Hod to Tiferet, where the soul

seeks entry into the body. The bottom six paths are the home of personality; the middle eight paths are all about the higher self. This is the path where the shaman or healer works with the spirits of natural objects and locations to bring healing and fertility and to uncover the hidden knowledge nature can provide." As Jacob looked up, he noticed Esair writing notes in his leather-bound notebook, and he smiled at him. "Netzach to Tiferet is the path of transformation. The soul is now yearning to be completed and perfected. We are shaping ourselves to learn and go on and teaching ourselves how to live and survive in this world," Jacob added. "The pure energy of the soul is split along this path into the rainbow light that contains all feeling."

"Kind of like a prism as it splits the light into many colors," said Joshua.

"Correct," said Jacob. "Exactly like that. Moving on, Tiferet to Geburah is the path of discipline. Divine energy brings us the lessons we must learn and which we need. The lessons are not always easy or pleasant, but our duty is to learn and seek return through perfection."

Gersham raised his hand asked, "Return to where, Jacob?"

"Where do you think, Gersham?"

Gersham thought long and hard and replied, "To God?"

"Yes," said Jacob. "That's the right answer." Happy with himself, Gersham was quiet and Jacob pressed on.

"Another path that is important to us is Netzach to Chesed. This is the path of progress. This is a place of natural progression, where the limitless bounty of God's love is passed on. The seasons turn here, the stars form overhead, and all living things have their rightful and proper place in this cycle." Jacob looked straight at Gersham to see if there were any questions. There was nothing but silence, so Jacob continued.

"Another path is Tiferet to Chesed. This is the path of acceptance. Tiferet is a place of great beauty, but God's love is much greater than here. This path requires an open mind when one doesn't know how to proceed. This path appears odd, but appearances can be deceitful, and it leads to huge storehouse of love and wisdom. To travel the adjoining path, Yod, is to turn away from the happy people and walk this path alone. The only way to complete this path is to put all thoughts and pride aside and open-mindedly accept help and advice that you feel you don't want or need."

Jacob looked up at the sky to figure out what time it was. "Is everyone OK?" he asked. "I want all of you to stand up and spread your legs apart, and with both arms, reach for the sky. Rid yourselves of any pain or tiredness that you have. Breathe in the fresh air that God has created for you today." They all followed Jacob's advice and totally felt refreshed and ready to continue. To cure their hunger, Jacob passed out some fruit, which was received with much gratitude.

"OK," said Jacob, "that felt good." He continued on. "The next path is Geburah to Chesed. One thing to know here is that I'm not going in order. I'm giving you the paths that I think are very important and which are important to me. Now, this is known as the path of restraint. The force that powers the soul lives here. It is the energy of life itself. It is also the home of the angelic beings, the executors of God's will and love. To walk this path, you must accept and face your deepest fears and, in doing so, learn how to control your basic instinct and behaviors.

"Next we have Geburah to Binah. This is the path to the pure power of God. This is the path that can lead the soul back to God. To travel along this path, you must pass through the fifty gates of understanding. You then must pass seven tests of vice by possessing the right thoughts and conduct. When each of the forty-nine tests have been passed, the fiftieth gate opens and passage to God becomes possible."

"Wow, incredible," said Esair. "So even the righteous man must pass those tests."

"That's correct, Esair. That's correct," said the Baal Shem. "Continue on, Jacob. It's starting to get late." Jacob nodded his head and went to another path.

"Chesed to Chokmah is the path of revelation. Here is the voice of God, excitement, and glory. It is said that God divided the light from the darkness here, the day into night. This is a path of true wisdom, an exciting place where the unexpected can lift the mind toward enlightenment. To travel down this path, you must first silence the inner voice of your mind and soul. Only then will you be able to hear the true voice of the divine wisdom that will guide you."

"Wow," said Gersham. "Will this voice give me what I need to turn a lump of clay into a living being?"

The rabbi looked down at Gersham with major concern in his eyes. "There is much more to the Tree of Life and its paths than creating life from nothingness. Learn this, and everything else will take its place."

"It's getting late," said Jacob as he looked over at the Baal Shem. "We will pick up here on Tuesday morning. Be back here at around nine." As the students put out the fire and headed home, Jacob stayed back with the Baal Shem.

The rabbi said quietly to Jacob, "Please keep an eye on Gersham. He is a very smart young man, and all this talk of creating a golem, life from nothingness, is starting to worry me a bit. We must keep him on the right path, and hopefully he will forget going down this darker path."

"I understand, and I will watch him. I am concerned about him too," said Jacob. With this understanding, the two of them left the forest and took a leisurely walk home.

THREE

Jacob got home, walked up the steps to his front door, and went inside. His wife, Maya, was waiting for him and preparing dinner. Jacob walked over, kissed her cheek, and then deposited himself in his favorite chair and nodded off. When dinner was about ready, Maya walked over and whispered gently to her husband to let him know it was time to eat. Jacob opened his eyes and smiled.

"Long day?" asked Maya.

"No, not really," said Jacob. "The Baal Shem and I are worried about Gersham, a fourteen-year-old in our study group. He has so much to learn, yet he is obsessed with the darker side of the Kabbalah."

"You mean like dark magical spells and amulets?"

"And more. He is very determined to know how to make and give life to nothingness, a lump of clay or earth."

"A golem!" screamed Maya.

"Yes, yes, a golem," whispered Jacob.

"You're not going to teach him, are you, Jacob?"

"I'm not planning on it," said Jacob. "However, the rabbi and I are both going to keep an eye on him. We can't stop him from his desire to learn, but we can help him down the right path."

"Understood," said Maya. "Let's go have a nice dinner. I made your favorites, potato pancakes and herring in wine sauce."

"Sounds great," said Jacob as he walked to the dinner table.

Morning came, and the sun was out. People in the community were out and about, as the temperature was close to forty degrees.

Jacob and the Baal Shem met in the front of the synagogue by the large wooden doors and greeted each other.

"Shalom, Rabbi," shouted Jacob.

"Shalom, Jacob," answered the rabbi. "The others are at our meeting place waiting for us."

"They can wait a few minutes longer," said Jacob. "At dinner the other night I spoke to Maya about Gersham. I decided it would be hard to stop Gersham's learning about spells and such, and if we forbid it, he may get upset and go down the dark path himself. So I suggest we continue to watch and help him to stay on the right path."

"Good suggestion, Jacob. Let's head over to the fire. It should be going by now."

FOUR

Jacob and the Baal Shem arrived at a beautiful fire and a group of waiting students.

"Everyone, sit down," said Jacob. "We'll try to finish up the paths of the Tree today." With the beautiful fire ablaze, Jacob started.

"The next path we can take is Tiferet to Chokmah. This path connects the pure energy of the divine with the beauty and peace of the soul, and as such represents God's breathing life into the universe per the entire Tree. Walking this path is an act of faith in God. Without this path there can be no peace in the face of laughter and no progress toward Chokmah's pure excitement.

"Binah to Chokmah is the path of ecstasy. It is the union of the mother and the father in an explosion of divine perfection and love." Jacob looked down at his students. "Well, you all had to come from somewhere. Only a mother and father's love for one another can produce beautiful, smart, and inquisitive men like you.

"Tiferet to Kether is the path of trial. The link between head and heart is uphill all the way. This is the longest of all the paths. It is the link between the immortal soul and the word of God itself. Any baggage or imperfections will weigh you down so heavily that the journey will almost be impossible. Yet all you need to do to complete this path is to innocently accept the unity of all mind.

"The path from Binah to Kether," Jacob continued, "is the path to awareness. This is a sanctuary in which the divine can dwell, the house of prophecy and vision. From here, all things can be seen or known. To walk this path is to see all but be touched by nothing."

"The path of Chokmah to Kether is the path of faith. This is the moment the universe was born. To walk this path, you must have total trust in God, accepting that it is unknowable. To have such total awareness of the universe is that there is no sense left of self. Aleph, as this path is known, says, "I am," and says it so loudly and precisely that even *I* and *am* lose their meaning.

"Lastly," said Jacob, "I'm going to teach you about the three veils of God. The Kabbalists say that the true face of God is hidden behind three veils. Each one is impenetrable and infinite. The veils soften the force of God's likeness so that his majesty does not sweep aside all divisions within the Tree of Life and bring about the end of the universe. They are beyond our understanding and awareness. There is no path to them and no way to cross them. They are a symbol of our limited ability to understand God. Veil one is a solid arc. It is known as Ain Soph Aur, which means "limited light." Veil two is shaped the same; however, it is represented by a line of long dashes. It is called Ain Soph, or "limitless infinity." Veil three is located behind the other two veils. It is represented by a line of short dashes called Ain. This means "limitless void." All three veils are really just one veil and are inseparable. The veils are forever outside the understanding of even the most enlightened human minds." At this everyone in the group started asking questions. In fact, the five of them were all asking questions at the same time. Jacob held up his hands and quieted everyone down.

"Talk together and figure out what one question you'd like to ask. Time is running very short." They all quieted down and spoke amongst themselves.

Esair finally stood and looked at Jacob. "Jacob, if we cannot see God with our own eyes, how do we all know he is here and with us?"

The Baal Shem looked down at the group's quizzical faces. "Look around," he said. "What do you see?"

Abraham, who was standing against the tree, looked up and said, "I see trees, birds, plants, streams, and all kinds of life. I see us and know that we were made in God's image."

"That's right," said the rabbi. "Joshua, what do you see?"

Joshua stood up and answered, "I see living things. I see the fire blazing as if it were alive and keeping us warm." He then looked at Gersham, who was dying to say something, and sat back down.

"All right, Gersham," said the rabbi. "What do you feel?"

Gersham looked up and said, "I feel life with each and every breath I take. I feel love for my parents and love for the people in this group. I feel love for our community."

"Excellent, Gersham, that is a great answer."

Lastly the rabbi looked at Esair. "Esair, what do you want in this world?"

Esair looked straight into the fire, then up at the rabbi. "Rabbi, I have all I want. I have friends, family, food, and a home to keep me and my family warm. I have clothes on my back. I have all of you, my group of friends that I study with. And I have faith in our community and the knowledge that God takes care of all of us."

The Baal Shem and Jacob smiled. "Each one of us and all of us see God in many ways. We feel good in many ways and we thank God for all he has given us. That's how we can see God. I am very proud of you all." The rabbi then smiled a large smile.

"I must go on a journey and Jacob will become the leader and rabbi of our temple. Please see him with your questions and thoughts, and I shall see everyone when I return."

"Where are you headed, Rabbi?" asked Gersham.

"On a very spiritual journey. Don't worry, my friends. I'll be back before you know it."

Everyone formed a line and gave the rabbi hugs and prayers. Then they all walked home to ponder what they had learned.

FiVE

The next day came around quickly. After a restless night of sleep, Gersham got up and sat on the edge of his bed. He opened his curtain and looked outside to see the sun starting to rise over his community. It was still cold out, but it looked like it was going to be great day. While the rest of his family slept, Gersham got dressed and quietly walked downstairs and out the front door. It was still early, and it seemed that he was the only person up and moving. He continued walking till he approached the temple.

He walked around to the back, and as he predicted, the back door was unlocked. Gersham looked around and then went inside. Knowing his way, he walked into the rabbi's study and gingerly closed the door. He left the curtains to the study closed and lit a large candle for light, which was plenty as Gersham made his way around the study. Gersham noticed the large tapestry hanging behind the rabbi's desk. It practically covered the entire wall. Curious, he went behind the tapestry and found a door halfway down the wall. He knew he was onto something, but he didn't know what. All he knew was that if creation out of nothing was possible, he'd hopefully find it in the rabbi's study. He slowly opened the door, lit the candle on the wall, and noticed a long stairway heading down into the basement. Gersham slowly descended the steps, counting each one as we went. Eighteen steps. *Chai*, or "to life," he knew from his studies. Within the Jewish faith the word *chai* possessed both numerical and symbolic meaning. Numerically the number eighteen was universally tied to the word *life*. The word consisted of the eighth and tenth letters of the Hebrew alphabet, Chet and Yud, which added up to eighteen. Putting the letters together created the word *chai*. *Has to mean something down here*, Gersham thought. And with each step he took, the more nervous and excited he became.

Once at the bottom, Gersham continued his way down the short path. It was cool and damp. The walls were nothing but stone, and cool to the touch. After eighteen more steps down the stone corridor, he looked to his left and found another door. He looked back from whence he came, opened the door, and went inside, closing the door behind him. Still carrying the candle, he looked around and found a small wooden table and chair in the center of the room. He turned around, and his eyes almost popped out of his head with amazement. Across the opposite wall were old, dusty shelves that looked to be a library of very old books. As he went closer, he realized that this was no ordinary collection of books. This was the rabbi's private and secret library, consisting of books on the Kabbalah, amulets, and spells. He pulled out the book of spells and noticed there were spells of white magic and dark magic. There were healing spells. There were spells to help enrich a person's life, and spells to protect people from the evil eye or any other curse cast upon a person. There were also books dealing with creation, demonology, wizardry, and sorcery. *I could spend all day down here,* thought Gersham. Gersham was overwhelmed but remained calm as he sat down to read by candlelight.

Gersham spent a good part of the day learning all he could. He paid extra attention to the books on creation. He studied spells on creating life from nothingness, and he studied amulets and anything else he could get his hands on. Before he knew it, he faintly heard the bell ringing in the tower, which stood above the synagogue, and knew he had to get home. And then Gersham did what he never would have expected to do. He was hesitant, but he took the book on creation, tucked it into his coat, and left the rabbi's secret library. He quietly closed the door behind him and hurried up the stairs back to the rabbi's study. He placed the candle back in its holder and reminded himself to replace the candle the next time he came. Gersham knew he had crossed the line, but it was too late to turn back. He didn't want to leave anything behind that would look suspicious. He looked out from behind the tapestry and saw no one. He hurried out of the study and out the back door of the temple. He went home as if nothing had happened that day, ran up to his room, and hid the book on a shelf behind his other books. Gersham sighed and then went down to dinner, praying the rabbi would be gone longer than anticipated, and that Jacob knew nothing about the library.

After a good dinner of lamb and potatoes, Gersham told his parents he had studying to do while the rabbi was away and ran upstairs. His parents continued to clean up after their meal. They were very proud of him and at times even bragged to their friends about what a great scholar their son had become.

Gersham spent the whole night studying and writing down notes, his thoughts, and ideas from the book of creation. When he was finished, he knew he had to go back to the library and replace the book he had taken and bring home the book of spells and amulets. Gersham lay back on his bed and fell asleep. He dreamt many a dream and about six hours later woke up in a cold sweat.

"I really need to make this happen," he said to himself. "I will sneak out tonight and go back for the book." Gersham was becoming obsessed to the point of no return.

SiX

The following morning found Gersham working at the family bakery, doing what he did best: getting challahs ready for baking. By mid-afternoon, Gersham had finished his quota of challahs and took out a broom and began to clean up the mess in the back of the bakery between the prep tables and the brick ovens used for baking breads. Wiping the sweat from his brow, he looked up and couldn't believe his eyes. It was snowing harder than he had ever seen it snow before. He quickly found his dad and closed the shop for the day. Making sure the bakery was secure, they locked the door and went home.

The snow kept falling hard. In the last two hours the small town had accumulated six inches and it was still falling hard. The snow was fluffy and wet and made for great snowballs. The younger kids came out and formed teams for the great snowball fight. Even some of the older kids joined in. Esair, Joshua, and Abraham led their team to victory.

Joshua noticed Gersham and his father walking home from the bakery. "Come over and join our team, Gersham. It seems we can't be beat."

"Sorry, guys, need to get home. I've got a lot of studying to do."

"What are you studying?" yelled Joshua. "It can't possibly be as much fun as this."

"You'd be surprised, Joshua. I'll catch up with you guys tomorrow."

By this time, it was starting to get dark and everyone started heading home. Cold and tired, everyone was looking forward to having a warm meal and reading by the fireplace.

But not Gersham. It was still snowing hard, but he had to get back to the secret library.

Gersham seemed to swallow his meal whole. He had to return the book on creation and borrow the Book of Spells and Amulets. He bundled up and told his parents that he needed to check the temple and make sure everything was in order, and then he sped out through the front door. He walked to the temple as fast as he could, lifting each leg up as he walked through the deep snow, like he was marching. He made it to the temple and went to the back door. Again, he looked around—right to left, left to right, and behind. Satisfied nobody would see him, he stomped his boots to get the snow off and went inside. He crossed the rabbi's study and ducked behind the huge tapestry covering the wall. He found the door, opened it, and lit the candle. He walked down the stairs, counting eighteen steps, and after eighteen more steps found the door on the left and went inside. He replaced the book back onto the shelf and grabbed the Book of Spells and Amulets. He tucked it away into his coat and headed out the door of the library. All of a sudden, Gersham froze. He was hearing scattering noises behind him. He quickly turned around and saw two large rats scampering down the hall. Gersham let out a huge sigh and quickly ran up the stairs, put the candle back in its holder, ran out the study to the back door, and headed for home.

Gersham couldn't sleep, not even for a minute. His heart was pumping faster with excitement. *I can't believe I did it again. I slipped in and out, and now I have the book that I hope will bring this all together*, thought Gersham. *Tomorrow I will go see the others and let them know all about my plans.* As he sat on the edge of his bed, his mind racing with anticipation, he removed his clothing, crawled into bed, and finally fell asleep.

SEVEN

Jacob abruptly woke up the following morning with thoughts that something was terribly wrong. He washed and dressed, ate breakfast, and still couldn't shake off this feeling of dread. The snow had stopped early that morning, and Jacob put on his coat and walked to temple. The air was brisk and the wind was slightly blowing in his face, but to Jacob, it felt refreshing. He arrived at the temple and, like Gersham, went in the back door. But this morning Jacob noticed the door was still partially opened. After making sure the door was completely closed, he walked directly to the main sanctuary to see if anyone was inside praying. "Nobody," he said. He then walked down the hall toward the rabbi's study. This door was slightly opened too. Jacob was beginning to get concerned.

Something is not right here, he thought to himself. As he looked about the room, he also noticed that the tapestry behind the rabbi's desk was not hanging straight as it always had. He rushed behind the tapestry and opened the door to the eighteen steps down. Jacob did know about the rabbi's private library. In fact, up to this point Jacob thought he was the only one. He went to light the candle and realized that the candle was burnt down to just about nothing. Jacob was sure that someone else had come across the library, and he knew that he had to find out who. Jacob opened the top drawer of the rabbi's desk and put a new candle in its holder, lit it, and walked down stairs. He came to the library, and his fears were dead on. Again, the door was not closed tightly. He went inside and looked at the shelves of books. To his dismay he noticed the Book of Creation was put back in the shelf upside down. And then Jacob noticed that the Book of Spells and Amulets was gone. He went book by book, shelf by shelf, and realized that the book was not in its proper place. In fact, the book was nowhere to be found. Jacob left the library and locked the door behind him. He came back upstairs and put the candle back in its holder, carefully blowing it out and marking the length of the candle. Then Jacob straightened out the tapestry and sat in the rabbi's chair to meditate and think.

"The two books taken were on creation and spells and amulets," he thought. "Who would want . . ." And then it hit him.

"GERSHAM!" he shouted. "He's wanted nothing more than to create life out of nothingness. I've got to find him!"

Jacob ran out of the temple and over to the family bakery. The bakery was closed. He then hurried over to Gersham's house, but Gersham wasn't there either. *Damn, where is that boy?* wondered Jacob.

EiGHT

eanwhile, Gersham had gathered up Esair, Joshua, and Abraham, and the four of them went into the woods, to their meeting place, but did not build a fire.

"I'm freezing," said Abraham.

"Sorry, we can't light a fire today. I don't want to attract anyone to our whereabouts," replied Gersham.

They all sat down on their tree stumps and Gersham began.

"First and foremost, what I'm about to show you and talk about is to be kept secret at all costs by each one of you. If you can't swear on your life, then you must leave now, and don't mention this to anyone you meet." The three others all looked at each other and swore their oaths. Gersham smiled. He began to tell the others what he had done and the books he had found.

"I have been sneaking out to the rabbi's study and I found his secret library. You all know how badly I want to try and create life from nothingness, and I believe that I've found a way to do this."

"Wow!" gasped the others.

"That's fantastic," said Esair. "But aren't you afraid someone will find out about this?"

"No, not at all. I took many precautions and did my best to cover my tracks."

"When and where do we start?" asked Esair.

"Let's think this through," said Abraham. "What are the consequences if this should happen to work? I'm not saying it will, but by a slight chance it does, what then?"

Gersham had never thought about this before. His mind wasn't sure it would work or not. "Well, if it works, we'll worry about it then."

Esair chimed in again. "How and where will we go to make this happen, to create this so-called golem?"

Joshua spoke up. "I know a place about a mile north of here. There is a small little hut-like place hidden behind some growth in the woods that makes it hard to find. Kind of like a rundown church of some kind."

"Take us there," said Esair.

So the four of them headed north through the forest to find their small rundown hut.

On their way, Gersham said, "There are words and meanings I must share with you. I wrote these notes down so I wouldn't have to carry the books out here. Let's start with an amulet. An amulet is a material object on which a charm has been written, or where a charm or spell has been cast. People wear these to protect themselves from evil or black magic and to bring them luck."

"What's a charm?" asked Joshua.

"A charm is a chant or incantation recited to produce either a good effect or a bad one. Now, a spell may be written or spoken and involves the use of magical incantations, rituals, and symbols. The magician or sorcerer cast a spell in order to curse, injure, or bring on what he desires. The book of spells and amulets also told me that casting spells was revealed by Satan himself to his devotees and passed down through the ages. And the forces of darkness are obliged to act on behalf of anyone if they chant the words correctly. Spells and charms are cast for any reason desired: to give strength, to kill an enemy, to protect from evil, or to be successful in love. If the spell is chanted correctly, a person may be able to bring back life from the dead." Again, the three looked at Gersham.

"Unbelievable," said Esair. "But do you really think you can create this life from nothingness?"

Joshua looked up. "There, on the left, there's the hut I told you about." All of them, excited and cold, walked over to the hut. They looked through the small window and saw it was empty and had been abandoned for quite some time. Gersham then walked briskly to the front door and went inside. The others followed one by one into the darkness of the old hut.

NiNE

The small hut was empty, except for an altar up front and a religious cross behind it nailed to the wall.

As the boys looked around, Joshua said, "I can't believe this little place is still standing."

"Right, I know," said Abraham. "I wonder who owned this little place and who prayed here. This definitely was a small church for somebody."

Gersham interrupted the conversation. "We don't have a lot of time to waste, so let's get started. First, let's build a shape in a human form. There's plenty of clay and mud on the floor here."

"Where should we build our human form?" asked Esair excitedly.

"Where else?" answered Gersham. "Let's create him on the altar."

"That's a perfect place," said Esair. "Now are we really sure,

I mean absolutely sure, we want to do this? We have to think of the consequences this will have if it works."

Gersham looked up at Esair. "Are you scared? Do you want to back out, or do you want to have some fun?" asked Gersham.

As Esair thought, he reluctantly shouted, "Let's have some fun!"

"OK then." And the boys gathered up mud and clay from the floor of the hut and formed a human-looking form. They did not notice how dark it was getting outside. Each one of them was consumed with the idea of creating this human form as exact as he could.

"Should we put some clothing on him, or at least a hat?" asked Joshua, trying to be funny and add a little levity to the situation.

"No," said Gersham. "However, I have my amulet we can place in his chest for good luck."

When they were finished joking, Gersham took out his notes of the different spells he had written down.

"OK, here we go. Form a circle around our mud man and join hands." The boys formed a circle, joined hands, and Gersham began chanting the words he had found in the Book of Spells. Gersham spoke the words of the chant clearly and with authority, over and over again. Each time, his voice continued to get louder and more powerful. It was like he was in a trance, and Gersham's voice seemed to change. His voice got deeper and more intense as he kept chanting. Lightning started to flash in the sky uncontrollably, as if the sky was opening up to Gersham's will. Thunder started, as if it was talking back to the boys as a warning against what they were doing.

And then the sky opened up as rain started pouring down in buckets. The boys were extremely frightened and broke the circle. It was raining so hard that the boys were stuck inside the small chapel. The rain was coming down so hard that Abraham, who was standing by the window, couldn't see two feet in front of him. The boys couldn't have left if they wanted to. They were all frightened as could be, except for Gersham, who kept chanting and chanting. All of a sudden, Abraham leaped away from the window and tackled Gersham onto the dirt floor. Gersham stopped chanting. The lightning started to dissipate. The rain slowed down to a drizzle. Gersham opened his eyes and looked up at Abraham.

"Did it work? Did we create life from nothingness?"

No one answered until Abraham softly and stiffly said, while wiping the dirt off his robe, "Let's get the hell out of here, now!"

Gersham turned around to see their mud man still lying on the altar, lifeless as could be.

Turning away slowly, Gersham answered, "Yes, let's get out of here."

The rain had stopped, and the four friends had a muddy walk home. It was a long and silent walk home.

No one spoke until Gersham quietly said, "I can't believe my chant didn't work."

Joshua jokingly answered, "What do you mean it didn't

work? You managed to bring life to the sky. You made lightning and thunder. You made the sky open up with buckets of rain. So it wasn't a total loss."

All of a sudden, everyone started laughing, except for Gersham.

What did I do wrong? he thought. *What did I do wrong?*

TEN

Everyone got home safely. It was almost midnight, and Gersham removed his dirty clothes, washed up, and went to bed. As he lay there looking up at the ceiling, a strong wind came through his open window, and he shivered violently. A few minutes later, he heard one of the strangest shrieks he had ever heard. It was so strange that he jumped out of bed and ran to the window. He kept looking back and forth down his street but saw nothing. As Gersham kept looking down from his bedroom window, he continued to hear the strange sounds, which felt like an eternity. All of a sudden, the moaning and shrieking stopped. He quickly closed the window and got back into bed, pulled the covers up over his head, and closed his eyes.

Must have been the wind, he thought to himself. *It had to be the wind, or was it?* He thought the same thought over and over again in his head till he fell asleep. But he did not sleep soundly. What he had done gave him horrible nightmares.

The sun rose the next morning and the temperature was mild and truly comfortable. Esair got up, dressed, and ran over to Gersham's house. Joshua and Abraham were already there.

"Did you hear those strange sounds last night?" asked Esair.

"We all did," said Joshua. "The shrieks and moans were scary as hell. I couldn't sleep through all of that noise."

"That means if we all heard it, I'm sure many others heard the noises as well," Abraham said with worry in his voice.

Gersham spoke up. "I'm sure it was just an animal in the woods who got badly hurt, so it's not much to worry about."

"I highly disagree with that statement!" said Jacob. The four boys looked up and turned around slowly. There, blocking the doorway to Gersham's room, stood Jacob, with a sorrowful look on his face.

"That was no animal we heard last night. What the hell did you boys do?" He stared at Gersham, who looked away. Abraham looked up and pointed his finger at Gersham.

"He made us do it," he cried softly. Gersham stood up quickly.

"All of you wanted to join me in this!"

"We all were just trying to watch you and keep you out of trouble," yelled Abraham. "I wish we would have stopped you before you began. It definitely scared the hell out of me."

"Us too!" shouted Joshua and Esair.

A huge fight, full of yelling and shoving, broke out between the boys.

"Enough!" yelled Jacob. "You are all in this together. You all participated in this monstrosity, and you will all have to suffer the consequences. Especially you, Gersham." Jacob shook his head. "I know it was you who broke into the rabbi's office and snooped around. I know it was you who found his way down to the secret library. And I know it was you who removed two books from the shelf. The Book on Creation and the Book of Spells told me it was you. Not replacing the candle told me it was you. I am very disappointed in you, Gersham. I'm disappointed in all of you." Gersham continued to stare at the floor, speechless. He knew he should have not attempted this without the proper supervision. Gersham put his hands over his face and began to sob.

ELEVEN

Jacob looked at each of his students, asking questions. Gersham showed Jacob the chant he had kept repeating over and over again. Esair told Jacob about the thunder and lightning and how hard it had rained, and how when Gersham chanted over and over again, his voice became deeper and deeper. Jacob just stood there staring at Gersham.

"You better be telling me the truth, because there was no thunder and lightning here. There was no rain. It hasn't rained here for at least a week."

"We swear to you, Jacob. We are telling you the truth," Abraham said. "I finally jumped away from the window and tackled Gersham to the ground. The chanting stopped and so did all the lightning, thunder, and rain. While Gersham was chanting, he became someone else. That's why I got scared and tackled him. It worked because he blinked his eyes over and over and looked at me, asking, 'Did it work? Did it work?'"

"You said there was a window. Where did you perform your ritual?" Abraham told Jacob about the small rundown chapel one mile north of their meeting place.

"Take me there! Now!" The boys walked in single file out the door past Jacob, and silently they all walked together to the forest and then headed north to the small hut. They all went inside.

"Yeah this used to be a small church," said Jacob. "But whose, I'm not sure. Where's the body you made of mud and clay?"

Gersham walked up to the altar. "It's right . . . It's gone!" Gersham stared down at the outline left in the dirt and mud. "What is this, some kind of joke?"

"No, it's not a joke." Jacob came over and looked at the outline. He made a circle around the void in the dirt, knelt down, and touched some of the loose soil. "This is no joke. It looks like your chanting brought this thing to life and it's out there, somewhere. And we've got to find this thing before the rabbi gets back. Hopefully our mud man, or golem, will return to this place at night.

"It's the place he was created or born, so it may be a sanctuary to him. I will head back to the rabbi's secret library to see how we can defeat this thing. Gersham, your voice will have to be the one to control him, and if there is a chant to send him back to the earth, it will have to be chanted by you. I hate to say this, Gersham, but he may think of you as his creator or mother and seek you out. We'll have to protect you as well."

TWELVE

Gersham shivered uncontrollably.

"Jacob, I'm so sorry for what I've done. It was all in fun, and I really didn't think I could do it anyway."

"Uh-huh," Jacob said without compassion. "For the next few hours you will stay with me so I can keep an eye on you and protect you as well. If you run off, you are on your own. Got it?"

"Yes," said Gersham, staring at the ground. Jacob put his hand on Gersham's shoulder and squeezed rather tightly.

"None of the townsfolk can know about this, understand?"

Gersham nodded, and they both headed for home.

Later that afternoon, Jacob and Gersham went to the synagogue and entered the rabbi's study and closed and locked the door. "Well, since you know all about this private library, you might as well come with me." Gersham perked up, and together they went behind the large hanging tapestry and walked down the eighteen steps heading to the private library. Again, once inside, Jacob locked the door and pulled out the book of spells and charms. Jacob sat down at the small wooden table and began to study. Gersham joined him. Gersham showed Jacob which chant he had used to bring his golem to life. Jacob studied the chant, put his hands over his head, and moved his head back and forth.

"Well, you've outdone yourself this time, Gersham. This will be very hard to stop. Where is the rabbi when you need him?"

"Hopefully he'll return to us soon," said Gersham.

"Hopefully, but we can't wait for him to return. We have to destroy this thing now."

"You're right, Jacob. We need a plan to destroy this thing. There has got to be a way."

Jacob studied the book of spells for hours, page by page, chant by chant. Nothing made sense to him regarding how to destroy this mud man. All of a sudden, Jacob stopped, marked the page in the book, grabbed Gersham, and raced upstairs as quickly as he could.

"Your golem will have to wait for now. It's the Sabbath and I have services to lead." As they left the rabbi's office and went into the main hall, Jacob noticed people filing into the main sanctuary for services. "Go to the tower and ring the bell, Gersham. No time to waste."

Gersham went outside to the tower and started to ring the large bell, letting the village know it was time to greet the Sabbath.

While ringing the bell, he heard the worst kind of sound he had ever heard. *The same sound I heard from my window that night,* thought Gersham. When the bell stopped, so did the shrieking. When Gersham started ringing the bell again, the shrieking got louder and more intense. Jacob heard it too. Gersham turned around, and there was his mud man staring right at him. The mud man was the color of mud and earth, stood about eight feet tall, and had large glowing red eyes.

Geez, did you guys have to build him so tall? he thought. Gersham froze and stared back at the creature.

"Get out!" he yelled, but the mud man started to creep closer and closer. Gersham couldn't move. The mud man crept closer and closer but did not attack. All of a sudden Jacob rushed in, grabbed Gersham, and pulled him out of the tower, slamming the door and locking it. Gersham composed himself, still breathing heavily.

"He didn't attack me. He just crept slowly toward me after I yelled, 'Get out!' I think he hates the sound of the bell. He shrieked when I rang it and stopped when it was silent."

"He recognized your voice, Gersham, but you can't trust it. He might have ripped you to shreds when he got close enough. You're lucky I heard the shrieks too. We have him locked in the tower, so let's start services like nothing happened."

Gersham breathing normally again, followed Jacob back into the sanctuary, and prayed for the next hour without an incident, without another sound.

THiRTEEN

Services ended without a hitch. The congregants were all in the great hall drinking wine and nibbling on fresh-baked challah bread made in Gersham's family bakery. After socializing, everyone went home to settle in for the night. Jacob and Gersham stayed behind and stopped Esair, Joshua, and Abraham from going home. Jacob spoke first.

"We have the golem locked in the tower. We must find a way to destroy it now!"

Their faces turning white, Esair yelled, "Are you serious? This is Gersham's problem."

"No, it's not, it's all our problem. Were you not in that little chapel helping to build this creature and lay it on the altar?"

"Yes," said Joshua. "We were there helping, so Jacob is right, we are all involved in this."

Abraham, with a worried look on his face, asked in a very stern voice, "How do we stop it? Do we use weapons against this thing, or are there chants to send it back to hell?"

Jacob sighed. "I'm not really sure. Tomorrow I will continue to study the Book on Spells, and I want you four to make or find some type of weapon so we can defend ourselves. Meanwhile I'll continue to study the books and, God willing, I will find our answer. I have got to find the exact chant to destroy our little friend here."

Gersham did his best to apologize to the others while in the woods looking for sturdy, long, thick tree branches to use for protection. Then they took out their sharp knives and whittled each branch till it had a very sharp end, which they hoped would be able to pierce their creation. Finally, Joshua stopped working on his spear and looked up at Gersham.

"Gersham, I'm tired and want to go home. Enough with the apologies already. This is all on us. The four of us have been good friends for a long time, and right now is no time to argue. We must stick together and try to defeat this thing we created. So let's finish our weapons and go home. Hopefully Jacob will find the chant to finish this thing off."

"Amen, brother," said Esair. "Let's finish these things and go home. I know it's the Sabbath, and I'd like to spend the rest of it with my family."

The four boys sat in a circle, finishing their spears. "Jacob will definitely like the weapons that we made, and I made one for Jacob to protect himself as well," said Esair.

"Great," said Gersham. "I'm cold, and if we're done here, let's get home before this night is over."

Everyone agreed and stood up. It started getting very windy. The trees creaked as their branches started to bend. The wind was ice cold and blowing straight toward them—so cold that they had to cover their faces so as not to freeze—and then they all heard the horrible shrieking and moaning they had heard the night before. The boys, scared stiff, readied their spears, formed a line, and headed for home. Joshua led the way while Abraham brought up the rear, constantly looking behind him so that nothing attacked them from behind.

"Please, Lord, please let us get home safely and in one piece," said Joshua.

"Amen!" whispered the others. "Amen."

FOURTEEN

The boys got back to the town safely, but they were very cold and shaky as well. They stopped and went inside the synagogue to get warm.

"Jacob!" they screamed. "Jacob, are you here?" No answer. They went to the rabbi's study; the door was locked. They looked in the library and study rooms—no sign of him. They crossed the great hall and went into the main sanctuary. Again, Jacob was not there.

"You don't think he went into the bell tower to take this monster on by himself, do you?" asked Esair.

"God, I hope not," said Gersham. "Well, we're going to have to go into the tower and make sure he's not a target for the mud man."

"Are you kidding me?" said Esair.

"Hey," said Gersham. "There's four of us and one of him. We are protected by our number and our spears."

The boys just stood there, still and silent.

"Let's go," said Joshua. "Follow me."

The boys walked around to the bell tower. They turned the doorknob, but it was locked.

"It's locked!" Abraham said with a sigh. Then from behind the stone tower, they all heard footsteps coming toward them. Quietly with each step, he approached the boys.

"About time you boys got back."

The boys jumped backward.

"Thank God it's you!" cried Gersham.

After Joshua caught his breath, he looked up happily. "You damn well scared us half to death! We thought you went inside to face the golem by yourself!"

"Not that stupid," said Jacob while laughing out loud. "Is that extra spear for me?"

"Yes," said Joshua as he handed it to him.

"Thank you, looks good and sharp. The golem is locked in the tower. I suggest we all head home for the night. All except you, Gersham. You will stay with me till we defeat this monster. We'll gather up your things and we will sleep in the rabbi's study, and in the morning, everyone will meet back here to plan how to defeat this thing you created. Now, all of you get home and lock your doors. Get some sleep. We have a hell of day coming up tomorrow."

Joshua, Abraham, and Esair headed for home, running in different directions. Gersham looked at Jacob. "I've got everything I need. Let's go to the rabbi's study and lock the door. I am very tired and could use some sleep."

Jacob and Gersham headed back into the temple and closed and locked the big wooden door.

"It's a full moon tonight," Jacob said as he locked the door to the study. "Let's get some sleep."

Then it came. The howling, the shrieking, and the moaning started to fill the nighttime air. It sounded like a pack of wolves howling at the moon. Gersham covered his ears and tried to fall asleep. Jacob sat behind the rabbi's desk, reading and studying the Book of Spells.

"There's got to be something in this book I can use to defeat this thing. There has to be something!" Jacob then rested his head on the book and he, too, fell asleep.

FiFTEEN

After four hours of interrupted sleep, Jacob woke up. It was still dark outside, and the wind was blowing up a storm.

"Wake up, Gersham."

"I'm up. It's hard sleeping on the floor. Need anything?"

"Listen and tell me what you hear."

"Nothing," said Gersham. "It's quiet as can be except for the wind outside."

"Exactly," said Jacob. "We've got to go into the tower!"

"I've got a bad feeling about this, Jacob."

"Just grab those spears and follow me."

They walked outside and went around to the tower, tightly holding their spears in front of them. Jacob pounded on the tower's heavy door. Nothing. No sounds, no howling, nothing. Jacob tried pounding once more. Again, it was silent. He pulled out his key and opened the door just slightly so as not to make a lot of noise.

"Be careful, Gersham. Keep very, very aware of your surroundings."

"I will," said Gersham.

Following Jacob, he entered the tower and looked around. Jacob lit a candle for more light. They looked around the entire floor of the tower, and it was empty.

"He's gone!" whispered Gersham.

"It certainly looks that way," said Jacob as he looked up the heavy bell rope to the top of the tower. Jacob noticed a lot of dirt on the rope and realized the golem had somehow climbed the rope and gone out the top of the tower.

"Our mud man is smarter than I thought, Gersham. Destroying this thing is going to be much harder than I thought."

Gersham, breathing easier, followed Jacob out of the tower and back into the temple.

"The others will be here shortly," said Jacob. "Try to get a little more sleep while I continue to study this book of spells and chants. There has got to be something here to destroy our golem."

Gersham lay down on the dusty wooden floor and went back to sleep. Jacob went down to the rabbi's secret library and looked for more help. While looking through all the dusty volumes, he began to check behind the books and noticed that behind the shelf on the floor was a very old book titled *Golems*.

"Where the hell has this book been? I've never seen this book before. Did the rabbi put this book on the floor behind the shelf to try and keep it hidden?"

Jacob picked up the book and sat at the small desk, bringing the lit candle closer so he could read. This book was not for the faint of heart. It was full of spells and chants separate from the other book of spells he was reading. As he opened the book, the dust on the floor began to swirl around and then abruptly stopped as Gersham walked in.

"Damn, Gersham. You scared the hell out of me. I thought I told you to get more sleep."

"I couldn't sleep worrying about things. What's going on down here?"

"I think I may have just found our answer to this problem, but I need more time to study this book. If you want, sit in the other chair and keep quiet. The answer to destroying this golem has got to be in here somewhere."

SiXTEEN

For the next two hours, Jacob studied every page in the book, desperately trying to find the one chant that would rid the world of this monster. He needed the exact chant to reverse the spell that brought this mud man to life.

"Damn, it's not here," said Jacob. "Gersham, I really wish you would have thought this through much more carefully before you started this. If we don't find a solution soon, others will be in danger."

Gersham just sat there with his head down, staring at the floor, and kept very quiet. Jacob went back to studying the book.

There has got to be a chant in here somewhere, he thought. "Let's go, Gersham. The others will be here soon, and we have work to do."

Jacob stood up and stretched his back. As he picked up the book to take it with him, a small flat piece of parchment fell out onto the floor. He picked up the old, yellowish piece of paper and looked at it in the candlelight. Jacob's face lit up with enthusiasm.

"Oh my God, this may be what I was looking for." He rolled up the parchment and tucked it inside his robe.

"Gersham, let's go. It's time for the others to show up." Gersham followed Jacob out of the secret library. Jacob locked the door and they headed up the eighteen steps to the rabbi's study. Jacob smoothed out the large tapestry on the wall and opened the door to the great hall. Joshua, Esair, and Abraham were sitting against the wall, waiting for them.

Jacob shouted, "Wow, are we happy to see you!"

"Where's Gersham?" asked Abraham.

"He's coming. I don't think he got enough sleep last night."

"I don't think any of us slept well either," said Esair. Jacob then proceeded to tell them of last night's adventure in the tower.

As Gersham came out into the great hall, Joshua spoke up jokingly and interrupted Jacob. "About time, Gersham. Did you get lost?"

The others laughed. Gersham did not reply. When the others stopped laughing, Jacob went on with his explanation.

"The golem's gone. I believe he climbed the bell rope and escaped from the top of the tower. We've got to find him," Jacob said with a hint of desperation in his voice. "Where would he have gone?"

Esair stood up. "When you think about it, I believe the

golem went back to the little chapel where he was born. That might be his safe place."

Jacob and the others agreed.

"Grab your weapons and follow me," said Jacob. "We're going to the chapel."

"Why?" asked Joshua. "Wouldn't it be better to go at night?"

"No," said Jacob. "It'll be easier to find and see him in the daytime. I have a feeling he likes the dark, so if Esair is right, our golem will be inside his home until darkness comes."

They all looked around at each other, agreed now was the time, and headed into the woods to the small rundown chapel where this all began. Gersham grabbed his weapon and led them quietly through the dark woods, past their place of study, to the little chapel one mile north. As they continued to travel north, the woods became darker and the cold winds started up again so that they had to cover their faces to keep warm. They kept on trudging forward through the thickness of the trees and chilling winds. As they got nearer to the chapel, it started pouring down rain.

"Damn," said Jacob as they kept trudging onward through the forest. "Enough with the rain already." Finally seeing the little chapel up ahead, Jacob stopped everyone to make sure they were ready to face this golem.

"If he's in there, we have to work together. Stay close to each other and be aware of what surrounds you. Are you ready?"

The others nodded. "We're ready." And quietly Jacob led them inside.

SEVENTEEN

O nce inside, Jacob lit a candle and the group formed a circle in the middle of the floor with their weapons at the ready. The candle gave just enough light for everyone to see. The circle moved slowly in a clockwise rotation. "He's not here," said Gersham.

"He's here somewhere," answered Jacob. "I can smell his foul stench. Check behind the altar."

"Who, me?" said Abraham with a shaky voice.

"No! I'll look behind the altar," replied Gersham. "After all, I created him."

"Keep your weapon in front of you, Gersham," whispered Jacob. "If you hear or see any movement, talk to it. Hopefully, he'll know your voice."

Gersham looked back at the others and slowly moved to the altar, one small step after another, till he reached the side and peeked around the altar. Gersham yelled a frightening yell to scare the golem, but it wasn't there. Relieved, he looked back at the others.

"He's not here. In fact, I don't think he's in this chapel right now." Everyone sighed in big relief.

"Damn," said Jacob. "This thing is going to be hard to defeat. We'll have to come up with a new plan. Let's head back to the temple, but be on your guard. He's out there somewhere." Joshua was the first one out, followed by Abraham, Esair, and Jacob. Gersham turned around at the door and gave the chapel one last look inside, then closed the door and joined the others.

Where is this thing? he thought. However, the golem made from mud and clay was inside. He had blended in with the dirt floor in the far corner so well that the group did not see him. But, Gersham was wrong. This mud man was in the chapel, hiding and undetectable.

Jacob led the group back to the synagogue, scratching his head yet holding his weapon out in front of him. As they walked through the woods, the wind seemed to die down the farther away they got from the chapel. To their dismay, it was a wasted day. The sun was starting to set and the cold embraced their town once more. As they approached the synagogue, they heard it: loud wails and shrieks along with moaning and howls. He was out there. But where?

"Let's go inside," said Jacob. "There has got to be a way to destroy this thing. I've got more studying to do."

EiGHTEEN

Everyone but Jacob left the temple and walked home together. They all heard the shrieking and howling carried by the wind to their small town. The boys were petrified hearing these sounds, but each one made it safely home. As Gersham got home, his parents were thrilled to see him. After all, they hadn't seen or heard from him in two days.

"Where have you been, Gersham?" his mother cried. Gersham knew he had to spill the beans and sat down with his parents. He told them the whole story and what he had done, taking full blame. His parents were in shock, not believing what they were hearing.

"How could you have done such a thing, Gersham? This is putting our town in peril!" shouted his father, Avram.

"I know, I know," said Gersham, looking down at the floor. "But Jacob is at the temple as we speak, trying to figure out what to do. I have faith in him."

"I guess this whole town needs to have faith in Jacob," said Avram. "How do we spread the word to others?"

"I'm sure the town is getting the information now from the others," said Gersham.

Gersham, who was beside himself, kept apologizing over and over again, when all of a sudden, things got very quiet. The howling and shrieking was heard very loudly throughout the town, and it seemed the golem was near. Everyone in the household started to shudder.

"Let's head down to the basement!" yelled Avram. Avram was a husky man about fifty-five years old and five feet eleven inches, with a gray beard and mustache. He had the hands and arms of a baker, big and strong.

He was pushing the family forward to the stairs down to the basement when a hard, repetitive knock came from the front door.

"Gersham, let me in," cried Jacob.

Gersham opened the door to his home and Jacob came in holding his wife close.

"Shut and lock the door, Gersham. You heard what I heard?"

"I think the whole town heard what we heard," said Gersham.

"I may have a way to destroy this thing, but we have to wait till morning!" said Jacob. "For now, follow your father down to the basement. We'll all be safe there, God willing."

Everyone huddled together, waiting for the horror to pass. Avram pulled out some blankets for them to wrap around each other and keep warm. Jacob pulled out the piece of parchment that had fallen from the book of spells and read it over and over again till he practically had it memorized.

"Gersham," he said, "when morning comes, go get the others and meet me at the synagogue. I may have a way to destroy our golem."

Gersham agreed, and everyone huddled together and fell asleep. All except for Jacob. He slept on and off, keeping watch to make sure they all remained safe. The howling had ceased, and it was quiet once again.

NiNETEEN

After a long, cold, and frightening night, everyone began to wake up, wondering if it was safe to go upstairs. Morning was here, but there was no sun, just a cold, gray, and windy day with scattered showers throughout the town. Jacob was the first to go upstairs. He crept up each step slowly till he reached the top. He looked straight ahead and then both ways. When he was sure it was safe, he called down to the basement and gave the all clear to come up. Avram was next to go up. He looked all around, and everything was in its place. With a big sigh, he also called everyone up.

Jacob looked up and saw Maya standing in the corner of the living space. He walked over to her and hugged her tightly. "You stay here, and I'll go check our home to make sure it's secure."

"I'd like to go with you," she said quietly.

"No, you'll be OK and safe here. I'll be back soon."

Jacob kissed her on the forehead and walked out the front

door. He ran all the way to his home. He had a horrific feeling in his body that told him something was wrong. As he reached his front door, he noticed it was ripped off the hinges and on the ground. He entered his home slowly, not making a sound. Jacob looked all around his home and shook his head in disgust. Something or someone had broken into his home and turned over all his furniture. His bookshelf was toppled over with all his books scattered all over the floor. Windows were broken out. Jacob was beside himself with anger. He cleaned up whatever he could and vowed that this was the end. He was filled with rage and vowed to put an end to this damn mud man. After doing his best to repair his front door, he went back to Gersham's. He found Maya sitting on the couch near the window. Maya was five feet four inches tall, with long black hair that reached her waist, and about one hundred pounds. She had beautiful brown eyes, and after seeing Jacob in the doorway, she knew something was wrong. Jacob came over and sat beside her and explained what he had found in their home. Maya's eyes started to tear as Jacob held her close and whispered in her ear.

"Thank God we weren't there last night. You're safe and I'm safe. That's all that matters."

Maya looked up at Jacob and smiled.

"I promise you," said Jacob. "We will destroy this thing. You'll stay here with Gersham's family where you'll be safe." The family agreed.

"Gersham!" yelled Jacob. "Where are you?"

Gersham was nowhere to be found. "He's not in his room, nor is he in the basement," said Avram. Jacob looked concerned.

"I'll round up his friends and we'll look for him."

"I'm going with you," said Avram.

"All right," said Jacob. He gave Maya a kiss and headed out to search for Gersham.

TWENTY

Gersham was alone as he walked to their big meeting place under the tall, wide tree in the forest. The tree was bare of all its leaves, but Gersham didn't care. He gathered up some wood and tree branches and built a fire in the pit. With a beautiful fire burning, Gersham sat on his tree stump and stared into the fire. He then fell asleep and dreamed.

All at once the fire rose to seven feet tall with flames shooting out in all directions. These flames turned into something human-like and the forms started dancing around the fire pit, calling out Gersham's name over and over. The forms were all dressed in white, and angel wings opened up from their backs.

"Gersham, Gersham," they sang. As he opened his eyes, he saw dancing white figures in front of him constantly calling his name. Finally, the dancing stopped. All the angelic beings combined to make one tall being. His wings spread out fifteen feet wide, and he looked down at Gersham. Gersham froze in place, unable to move as the being came closer.

"Gersham, you have done a horrific thing," the being said in a loud thunderous voice. "You've unleashed a monster who will destroy your community and maybe the world if it is not destroyed. Your spears and weapons will not destroy the golem. Using a crucifix, daggers, and silver bullets will not destroy the golem. Innocence will destroy the golem. Innocence will destroy the golem. Innocence will—" Gersham abruptly woke from his dream. There were no spirits. The fire was dying out, and Gersham stared into the glowing embers, shivering violently from the cold. Jacob saw the light glowing in the woods and yelled over to the others.

"This way!" Abraham, Joshua, and Esair ran over to the pit, and Esair took off his coat and placed it over Gersham.

"Let's get him back to the synagogue, quickly," said Esair.

And the boys lifted him up and walked back to the synagogue with Gersham in the middle, his arms draped over the shoulders of Joshua and Esair.

As they carried Gersham back to the temple, a loud, horrid shriek came from the woods. Jacob turned to make sure they were safe as the boys continued to make their way back. Once inside, the boys took Gersham into the main sanctuary and laid him on a long bench in front of the altar. Jacob closed and locked the door to the temple.

Why lock the door? he thought. *This damn mud man can rip off this door just like he did mine.*

There was no comfort within the temple walls. The boys placed a pillow underneath Gersham's head and covered him with blankets, and they prayed. There was an awful lot to pray for.

TWENTY-ONE

Jacob stayed with the boys in the main sanctuary. He kept thinking to himself, *Where the hell is the rabbi? Where the hell is the rabbi? If only he was here.* But unfortunately no one knew where he was. They hoped for their sake, and the town's, that he would come back soon.

Another day passed before Gersham began to stir. As he started to come back, he kept mentioning the word *innocence* over and over again. Abraham leaned over and spoke in a low voice to Gersham.

"Wake up, my friend. Wake up." Gersham began to open his eyes and saw the boys looking down at him.

"Where are we?" he said quietly.

"We're in the temple. Better yet, the main sanctuary," said Joshua.

Jacob rushed over and helped Gersham to a sitting position. "Good to have you back, my friend. We were very worried about you."

As Gersham rubbed his eyes to clear them, Abraham spoke. "Gersham, you kept saying *innocence* over and over again. Is there any meaning to that?"

But Gersham remained quiet and just stared forward at the ark. As he stared at the ark, his dream started coming back to him. He repeated the dream back to everyone in vivid detail, down to the last angel wing. Jacob thought, *What a dream*, but concentrated his own thoughts on the word *innocence*.

What can that mean? wondered Jacob as he excused himself to try to figure this out. Jacob went into the rabbi's study and closed the door. The others stayed with Gersham as he came back to consciousness.

"Can you walk, Gersham?" asked Joshua.

"Sure, I can walk." And Gersham got up to test his legs—a little wobbly, but he got stronger with each step.

The main sanctuary doors opened, and Jacob came rushing in. "I think I know what innocence means," Jacob said excitedly. "I've heard a story where a small, innocent child walked up to a golem to play. The golem picked her up and she pushed her hand into the golem's chest and pulled out the amulet that helped keep him alive. The golem fell to the ground and disintegrated into dust and dirt. That is how we will defeat the golem!"

"That's great," said Esair. "My question is, Where will we

get a small child, and why would the parents even agree to this craziness?"

"Good question," said Jacob. "Where and who. I don't want to put a small, innocent child in any danger; however, if we're going to destroy this mud man, we have got to figure this out."

"Is there a homeless child roaming around somewhere?" asked Gersham. "God knows, after all is said and done, I could be homeless," he said laughing and crying at the same time.

"Trust me, Gersham," Jacob said. "You won't be homeless after all this. If we fail, maybe the golem will take you in."

"Very funny," replied Gersham. "Let's just get this thing and put it out of its misery."

Jacob went back to the rabbi's study and thought long and hard.

I've got it! thought Jacob. *We've been studying Kabbalah. Let's use it to combat this golem. There's got to be a path we can use to solve this problem.*

Jacob left the study and went to round up the boys. They were still in the main sanctuary, waiting for Gersham to regain his strength. Jacob brought them all into the rabbi's study and locked the door. When Jacob had their attention, he began.

"We have studied the different paths that the Tree of Life offers us. The one path already taken is a path Gersham should not have taken you down. That was Geburah to Chesed. This path, as you recall, is the energy of life itself. You must accept and face your deepest fears and learn how to control them and your behaviors."

"Way to go, Gersham," said the others.

"Quiet, all of you," Jacob yelled. "You all followed Gersham down this path, so you are all guilty. I will try and lead you down the path of trial, Tiferet to Kether, and it is uphill all the way. This path is the longest of all paths and is the link between the immortal soul and the word of God. This journey will be almost impossible, yet all of you need to innocently accept what you have done and complete the task at hand. And that task is?" asked Jacob.

"To destroy the golem!" they all answered.

"That is correct, gentleman. Let's go out and finish this thing." They all jumped up at once and retrieved their weapons.

"Remember what I said. Those spear-like weapons will not destroy our mud man. They may help keep him at bay, but that's all they will do. It is getting dark, so tonight we will walk the community and try to keep the town safe from any destruction. We'll split up into three groups. Gersham will come with me. Joshua, you'll team up with Abraham. And Esair, Avram will join us tonight. You'll team up with him. Everyone agreed?"

"Yes," they all answered.

"Good, then let's go get Avram and get started."

Readied with their weapons, Jacob and the boys headed out of the temple and into the town. Avram came out his front door and locked it behind him. He joined up with Esair and walked the streets, looking to keep everyone safe.

TWENTY-TWO

The sun was setting behind the hills of the town. The wind started swirling, and with it, a chill filled the air. Everyone covered his face with his scarf to keep off the chill. All the teams walked in and out of the alleyways and in front of as well as behind every home and business. They all continued to keep vigil as the night went on; however, three hours into the walk, the winds picked up once again. This time, howling and screaming filled the air. The golem was out and about, and the three groups formed as one and huddled together. What was once a calm night had turned into a night of sheer terror.

Jacob remained calm as he looked around in all directions. "Tonight, this will end. We can no longer live in fear. There are six of us to only one. We have to surround this mud man, and I believe I have the spell to end its life. Listen closely to the howls and screams, and let's track him down and finish this."

"Amen," shouted the others.

"Then follow me," said Jacob.

Jacob led the others to the forest. Again, the wind started blowing with much more force, so much force that the group had to walk at an angle just to cut through the winds. As they reached their meeting place, they all took refuge under the large tree next to the fire pit. It was very quiet, so quiet it was as if everything had frozen in place and quit moving. Then they heard it—faint screams and howls—and Gersham knew exactly where they were coming from.

"We've got to go to the old church!" shouted Gersham. "He's there. I know he's there."

"Let's go," said Jacob. "Keep your weapons in front of you, your voices down, and be aware of your surroundings at all times." The group headed for the little rundown church, listening closely to every sound surrounding them. Jacob looked up and around. He could swear someone was following them. He kept looking back, but it was dark, and he couldn't see anything or anyone. They all reached their destination. Avram and Joshua kept watch outside the door as Esair, Abraham, Gersham, and Jacob went inside. It was so dark inside that Jacob lit a candle he had left there. Jacob smelled a strong stench and noticed two red glowing eyes in the far corner of the church.

"I see him," whispered Jacob. "Form a half circle around the altar with weapons at the ready." With Abraham on one end and Esair on the other, they made their way toward the glowing eyes in the corner. The golem screamed and jumped high in the air, over the group and into the opposite corner. The boys turned around and Jacob was already chanting the spell he hoped would destroy the golem. Over and over again he chanted, but the spell was not working. If anything, the golem was getting stronger, and the longer he lived, the more he was learning. The golem jumped toward Jacob, pushing him down in the mud with a force Jacob had never felt before. The golem headed for the door and broke the door from its hinges as he ran out into the forest. Jacob, still sitting in the mud, called to the others to help him out. The others, huddling next to the window, came over and helped Jacob up. They went outside to find Avram and Joshua hiding behind a large tree. Jacob was very upset. The chant did not work, and they were no better off than they had been before.

"I'm not done yet," yelled Jacob. "He's around here somewhere—I can smell him. I can feel his beady little eyes staring at us." As they began to comb the nearby area in the forest, they all stopped and readied their weapons. The wind began to blow again with a lot more force this time. The golem came out and let out a mean-sounding howl. Gersham lunged forward and yelled at the golem to return to whence he came, hoping the golem would recognize his voice as his creator. But no, the golem did not recognize Gersham's voice and readied to attack. Jacob ran toward Gersham, grabbed him by the arm, and pulled him back. The golem kept coming forward. He reached out for Gersham and grabbed his leg. He started pulling Gersham away from the others.

Gersham screamed, "Let me go, you damn monster!" But the golem would not let go as he continued to drag Gersham away. Avram ran into the golem to tackle it to the ground, but the golem just pushed him aside. He let go of Gersham and went to grab Avram.

Joshua tossed Avram a pointed weapon to help fight the golem. As he picked it up to defend himself, the stranger who Jacob sensed was following them flashed and appeared out of nowhere.

"Rabbi!" Jacob yelled. The others all took notice.

The rabbi positioned himself between the golem and Avram. He raised his right hand against the golem. Red, blue, and green lights of energy streamed out of his hand and held the golem motionless. Avram got up, grabbed Gersham, and ran back to the others. The rabbi then pointed his left hand toward the group, and bright yellow lights streamed out of his hand toward them and seemed to cover them with a protective shield of energy. The rabbi then changed himself into a small, innocent child, and with the energy holding the golem motionless, the rabbi moved closer to the golem and forced his hand inside his chest. The golem let out a scream so loud it shook the forest as if an earthquake were forming. The group all covered their ears to protect themselves from going deaf. The rabbi then pulled out Gersham's amulet from the golem, and everything went silent. The protective cover over the group seemed to dissipate. The golem disintegrated back into the ground. All was quiet again. And then another flash of light. The child became the rabbi once again. It seemed the rabbi was more than just a man. He possessed the power of the Kabbalah and now was a well-known wizard. The rabbi turned and stared at the group of scared boys.

"Esair, Joshua, and Abraham, go home to your families. Let your loved ones and community know the danger is over. And Joshua," he continued, "round up some of the builders and carpenters and have them repair Jacob's home if you please."

"Will do, and thank you," said Joshua. "I don't understand what I just saw, but I loved it." He then ran off with the others.

"Jacob and Gersham, walk back to the temple, more precisely my study. We have lots to discuss."

As the rabbi started off, Gersham pulled on Jacob's arm. "Am I in trouble, Jacob?"

"What do you think?" he answered. "What the hell do you think?"

TWENTY-THREE

It was an extremely quiet walk back to the temple. Jacob and Gersham followed the rabbi into his study and closed the door. The rabbi slowly walked to his desk and took a seat where he could look at the two of them. After a few minutes, the rabbi looked at Jacob and excused him from the study.

Jacob looked back at the rabbi before he left the study. "Be easy on him. He's just a kid."

Jacob left and closed the door behind him.

The feeling in the room was so thick you could cut through it with a sword. Gersham sat quietly in his chair, staring at the floor.

"Gersham," said the rabbi in a soft but gruff voice. "Tell me exactly what went on while I was gone. What did you do?"

Gersham looked up at the rabbi, then down at the floor once again.

"Gersham, just tell me the truth and we'll move on."

Gersham nodded and recounted the entire scenario to the rabbi, going through the story piece by piece and methodically in order. After he finished telling his story, tears began to run down his cheeks.

"Stay here. I'll be back in a couple of minutes." The rabbi walked out of his study and found Jacob praying in the main sanctuary. As he approached, Jacob looked up.

"Please join us back in my study, Jacob. We have things to go over."

Jacob stood up and followed the rabbi back into the study and again closed the door. A few moments passed, and the rabbi again stared across his desk at Gersham. "Gersham, what you did was extremely irresponsible and stupid. You broke into my office, snooped around, and found the door and pathway leading to my secret library. You took books home and put them back upside down and out of place. Those books are never to leave that library. Never! Then I understand you talked the others into helping you to create this golem. You were playing with fire, Gersham. Did you think forward at any time as to what you would do if your escapade worked and the mud man came to life? How were you going to destroy this thing?" The rabbi waited for an answer.

Finally, Gersham looked up. "I . . . I didn't think that far ahead because I really didn't believe this would work. It was stupid, and for this I truly apologize."

More moments of silence passed. The rabbi stood up and went to the front of his desk and leaned back on it in front of Gersham.

"Gersham, I knew what was happening here long ago, but I decided to do nothing unless things escalated to what they did. That was me Jacob sensed following everyone in the woods. Thank God I showed up because some of you could have been seriously hurt, or even worse, killed. I chose Jacob a long time ago to be my successor when my time is through. Hopefully that will be awhile. So much to see and so much to learn." Gersham looked up at the rabbi as the rabbi smiled down on him. "Jacob and I will teach you more of what you must learn within the Kabbalah. You have a very inquisitive mind and want to learn. However, you must promise never to pull a stunt like this ever again. It was very irresponsible, and you put many people at risk of getting hurt. And you must have my permission to go into my secret library at all times! Got it?"

"I got it," said Gersham. "I won't let you down again."

"All right, now both of you go back to your families and prepare for the Sabbath. We have a lot to thank the good Lord for."

TWENTY-FOUR

Gersham and Jacob left the temple and walked home. Gersham let out a huge sigh. "I can't believe that I didn't get his whole secret library thrown at me. I probably should have."

"I agree, Gersham. You are lucky in that respect. The rabbi treated you well this time. However, if it were me, I'd have tarred and feathered you for sure. And keep this in mind, Gersham: neither the rabbi nor I will give you a second chance."

"I understand," said Gersham. "The rabbi is very wise and understanding. From now on I will listen to my elders and discuss any questions I may have without acting on them first."

"Excellent," said Jacob as he smiled to himself. "Let's go home and get ready for the Sabbath. We have a lot to be thankful for."

As they walked home, the clouds spread open in the heavens and the sun came out to warm the little town. Gersham and Jacob saw it as a new beginning, and they were right. It most certainly was a new beginning.

ABOVE: The pure energy of the soul is split along the path of Nun into the rainbow light that contains all feeling.

ABOUT THE AUTHOR

Edwin M. Radin is an author who lives in Columbus, Ohio. He writes stories for children, teens, and young adults. His work includes *The Reluctant Penguin* series which includes *The Reluctant Penguin, Love and Ski Jumping,* and *Flipping out Without a Flipper*. He has also written an autobiography about his fourteen years in Scouting called *The Troop Clown*. He also invites you to visit his website at edwinradin.com.

www.ingramcontent.com/pod-product-compliance
Lightning Source LLC
Chambersburg PA
CBHW051931240626
47153CB00004B/1451